THE AMAZING Life of Birds

Also by Gary Paulsen

THE AMAZING Life of Birds

(The Twenty-Day Puberty Journal of
Duane Homer Leech)

As discovered by

GARY PAULSEN

WENDY
L A M B
BOOKS

Published by Wendy Lamb Books
an imprint of Random House Children's Books
a division of Random House, Inc.
New York

www.randomhouse.com/teens
Educators and librarians, for a variety of teaching tools,
visit us at www.randomhouse.com/teachers

Library of Congress Cataloging-in-Publication Data
Paulsen, Gary.
The Amazing Life of Birds : (the twenty-day puberty journal of
Duane Homer Leech) / as discovered by Gary Paulsen.
p. cm.
Summary: As twelve-year-old Duane endures the confusing and
humiliating aspects of puberty, he watches a newborn bird in a nest
on his windowsill begin to grow and become more independent,
all of which he records in his journal.
ISBN-13: 978-0-385-74660-1 (trade) 978-0-385-90897-9 (lib. bdg.)
ISBN-10: 0-385-74660-1 (trade) 0-385-90897-0 (lib. bdg.)
[1. Puberty—Fiction. 2. Self-perception—Fiction. 3. Schools—Fiction.
4. Birds—Development—Fiction. 5. Diaries—Fiction.] I. Title.
PZ7.P2843Ama 2006
[Fic]—dc22
2006004544

Printed in the United States of America

10 9 8 7 6 5 4 3 2 1

First Edition

To my son, James, in gratitude.
Having missed my own puberty,
because I lived through it,
watching you go through yours provided
a wealth of research material.
Thank you.

Foreword

I should have seen it coming.

A long time before it came I should have known.

I was six or seven years old and there was a girl living next door named Peggy. She was a year older than me and a lot stronger and we were wrestling and she held me down. . . .

Well, let's just say that some part of me didn't mind that she was holding me down even though she was a girl and I didn't like girls much. All of a sudden it seemed there was something about girls that wasn't all bad. I didn't know what it was but I should have known that this first feeling with Peggy Ollendorfer meant that down the road, later, I was in for a big surprise.

Afterward, when I was a little older, if you'd asked me what the surprise was like, I'd have said it was about like getting hit by a train.

Puberty.

Day One

This morning I became twelve years and one week old and last night I had a disturbing dream. Don't worry. It wasn't about ELBOWS.

I'd better explain. Lately I've been thinking a lot about the female body. Not in a weird or sick way but not in an artistic or medical way either. These thoughts aren't intentional. And they happen at the strangest times. I'll be sitting there, thinking of almost nothing, maybe about tightening my loose bicycle pedal, and there it will be, bang! Stuck in my mind: part of a woman's body. The part varies and I don't think it's necessary to say what it is—most readers can probably guess—but it's almost always embarrassing when this happens. Especially if you're sitting talking to, say, the math teacher Mr. Haggerston about equations and you look down and see not math equations on the paper but an enormous . . .

You get the idea. So to avoid problems, when this happens I force my mind to think the word ELBOW and I see an ELBOW and think about ELBOWS and wonder about ELBOWS and wish about ELBOWS. It helps. Sometimes.

Anyway, I had this disturbing dream about my father. In the dream he and I are sitting in a huge bird's nest watching a movie on television. The movie is *Ferris Bueller's Day Off*. Once a year since I was eight, my father makes me sit down and watch that movie with him.

He thinks it helps us to bond. Which isn't necessary because we get along just fine anyway. My father is a good guy, and my mother is really nice too, and I even almost get along with my older sister, Karen. I'd do better with Karen if she weren't demon spawn born in the fires of Hades, but she's been that way as long as I can remember.

But we have a good family. And I love them. Even my sister, I guess. We're all bonded as much as you can bond but still, once a year, my father sneaks out that old video. He and I watch it together and he proves once more that he Understands Young People and Knows What It's Like to Be a Boy.

As if.

All I can think when we sit there is in what

4

possible world would I get a Ferrari to drive around Chicago in with a beautiful girl on my arm and go eat in fancy restaurants while the principal of my school gets munched on by a Rottweiler? I can't even get my bike pedal tightened without thinking about ELBOWS.

But in the dream we're sitting in a bird's nest watching the movie and when it's over my father turns to me and puts his foot on my chest and says: "If you can ELBOW you can fly." Only of course he doesn't say ELBOW but another word, not a body part.

And he kicks me out of the nest.

Even in the dream I *can't fly*. I plummet down and down, falling and falling until I suddenly wake up and see that I'm in my room holding the pillow like it's somebody I know really well.

I know why I dreamed about the nest; a month ago two birds built a nest on the windowsill of my room, which is upstairs and in back by a tree. It seemed strange at first because there was the tree with lots of limbs, a much better place for a nest. But then I saw Gorm, the neighbor's tomcat, climb the tree and crawl out on the limb nearest the windowsill to try and reach the nest. Gorm is not the brightest chip in the matrix and instead of reaching the birds he redis-covered gravity, landing nicely on his feet but hitting as hard as a bowling ball because he's fat. In fact he kind of *looks* like a bowling ball. So that's why the birds used the windowsill. It's Gorm-proof.

One of them laid an egg and sat on it until it hatched into the ugliest little dirty brown bird I have ever seen. Then they started to feed him. Or her. They brought it bugs and more bugs and still more bugs, both of them flying back and forth all the time getting food for the little eating machine.

And now it's slightly bigger and still amazingly ugly, pink skinned and with bulging eyes. It has four brown scraggly feathers, two on the top of its head and two at its tail.

The thing is they really love the little bugger, and preen it and feed it and I'm sure would show it *Ferris Bueller's Day Off* if they could.

So that's where the nest comes from—I've been watching the Bird Family Channel for a month.

But why did Dad mention ELBOW? And why kick me out?

Wasn't it enough they'd named me Duane?

Day Two

Duane.

Homer.

Leech.

Think about it. When you look at it that way, each word separate, it's hard to see how my parents could have done it.

Look, we've all seen those shows on the Discovery Channel where they show a baby being born. There's a man in a hospital gown and a woman on a table and a lot of noise and sweat and there it is.

A baby. Looking actually a lot like the little bird on my windowsill, all messy and ugly.

Me.

And if they'd done a video there would be my

mother and my father smiling with love at me, all goobery and sloppy.

Defenseless, new in the world, not even a clue that someday puberty would come along and body-slam me.

And when they asked what my name would be, my father looked down probably all proud and loving and said:

"Duane.

"Homer.

"Leech."

I didn't have a chance—or maybe I would have had a slight chance, if I'd been name-lucky. People could have called me DH, or skipped the first name and called me Homes, which would be cool, or gone back to the first name and called me Duey, which isn't that good, but still on the edge of being all right.

But that's not what happened.

Oh—this morning the bird had one new small feather growing on the end of his right wing. Five feathers now. It's hard to look at him and see that someday he's going to fly. Or date or grow up to have a family so *he* can make *his* son watch *Ferris Bueller's Day Off*.

I decided to name the bird Connor. Which is what I wanted to be named. Or Steve, or Carl, or Clint . . . anything but Duane. Apparently I had a great-uncle or something named Duane and he did something important—nobody seems to remember what was so special about Duane the First. But the name was passed down and I got stuck. For my middle name, my father is a history nut and there was a famous Ancient Greek guy named Homer who did a lot of thinking, I guess, so Dad gave me that name so I would think a lot. And there must have been some wacko in our family who grew leeches once upon a time. Or maybe my family just evolved from bloodsuckers. . . .

So the little guy is always flapping that one-feathered wing like it's going to make him fly. That's about like me thinking I can ask Amber Masters to go to a movie with me.

Fat chance.

Not that she'd go. That's a given. She doesn't know I'm alive. I've never spoken to her. Or to any girl. Unless it's absolutely necessary, as in, "I'm sorry your hair is on fire," or "I'm sorry I slammed the tetherball into your face when we were in the second grade." I keep hoping Amber has forgotten both those incidents. I don't even know why I brought it up in this journal because I've never thought of asking a girl to do anything.

See? Another weird part of puberty.

But ask her? Never happen. It would be like the little bird flapping his one-feathered wing expecting to fly and instead learning all about plummeting the way Gorm learned about gravity.

Crash and burn. That's what would happen to me. Flames all the way down . . .

Doo-Doo.

There it is. The kiss of death. The nickname that came into my life in the third grade, came and stuck. Doo-Doo Leech.

My best friend, Willy Traverse, gave it to me by mistake. We were on the playground seeing if we could get the swings over the top and he looked over at me and said, *"Do it, Duey!"*

And three or four other kids who were there started yelling, *"Do it, Duey! Do it, Duey! Doo Doo Doo Doo . . ."*

So for the rest of my life I will be known as Potty Boy.

Doo-Doo Leech.

Flap, flap, flap . . . crash.

Day Three

I'm going insane.

Perhaps it's all part of this puberty thing but it's still not pleasant.

Totally crackers.

First, I wake up this morning like somebody gave me an electric shock. One second I'm sound asleep, drooling on my pillow, out, dead, not even dreaming, and the next I'm lying flat on my back staring at the ceiling counting the square tiles.

There are ninety-six of them.

And strange things are happening to my body. Parts are moving inside me, and coming outside me, and other parts are tightening up, and when I went down to have breakfast I looked at the rooster on the cornflakes box and bam, ELBOW. For a split second I thought the rooster had actually changed and turned into something else and I looked around wondering if anybody else had seen it but no. My father was sipping coffee over the sink, where he drinks it because he spills, and my mother was reading the newspaper while she ate a piece of dry toast because she worries about her weight, and my sister was sitting at the table wondering how to destroy the whole human race if she can't get her hair to look just . . . exactly . . . *perfect*.

So it was just me.

And the rooster.

And the ELBOW.

Then it was gone.

This morning I looked out at the birds as one of them brought the little guy a whole grasshopper, still alive, and stuck it in his mouth. It reminded me of the time Willy tried to get a whole hamburger in his mouth on a bet. It was just one of those White Castle bombs, not a big one, but still it was a mouthful and he almost choked to death before we figured out how to do the Heimlich maneuver on him. There were four of us and we each had a different idea about how it should be done until finally Pete Honer said, "He's turning blue," and we all just grabbed something and squeezed and he gacked it up and out. Pickles and all.

Except that the grasshopper was still alive and knew what was coming and spread his legs out across the baby bird's face and wouldn't go down until the parent bird used its beak to jam him down the baby's throat.

And then I thought maybe my life was not like the bird's but like the grasshopper's and that I was being eaten alive by puberty . . . but that got too weird.

So this afternoon after school I called Willy. He's still my best friend but his family moved to another town seven miles away, just far enough for us to be in different schools. We get together on weekends.

"Hi."

"Hi."

"This morning I woke up and counted the ceiling tiles."

"How many are there?"

"Ninety-six."

"Cool."

"Then I went down to breakfast and I saw ELBOW on the side of the cereal box where the rooster was standing."

"I've never seen it on cereal boxes. But once on the side of a bus and twice looking up at the clouds."

"This morning the bird on my sill ate a whole grasshopper."

"Cool."

"It made me think of that time you choked on the burger."

"Cool."

"Well."

"Well."

"Catch you later."

"Cool."

Willy's got puberty the same as me and sometimes it helps to talk things over.

It's good to have a friend.

Especially if you have a nickname like Doo-Doo.

I mean can you even *imagine* somebody named Doo-Doo driving a Ferrari around Chicago with a beautiful girl while a Rottweiler eats his principal?

I didn't think so.

Day Four

I woke up wondering what comes next.

This morning I was lying on my side and when my eyes opened I started counting the slats on the blind that slides down over my window.

Twenty-seven.

They go from side to side, not top to bottom, and lying on my side and trying to count them made me dizzy so I got out of bed and fell on my face halfway to the upstairs bathroom.

Good start.

Then I looked in the mirror over the sink and there was a zit in the middle of my forehead. Not just a small one. A giant. It looked like something in there was trying to get out and when I pinched it . . .

Well, enough of that. But now instead of a zit I

have what the TV would call a "suppurating wound." It isn't important to know what that means—just the sound of the words makes it work.

I have another zit on my chest which the shirt will cover but in the mirror my face looks like I tried to kiss a rotary mower.

I *can't* go to school. People will puke when they see me.

And that, journal reader, was the *high* point of my day.

I went down to breakfast and my sister said:

"Cover your face so I can eat."

"So it shows then? I was thinking nobody would notice it. . . ." Lame joke.

"What's that?" My father turned from the sink where he was drinking his coffee. "Oh."

"Maybe a Band-Aid," my mother suggested. "A flesh-colored one. It wouldn't show too much."

"Right." I turned slowly to the cornflakes box and sighed in relief. No ELBOW. Just the rooster. "Or I could just print up a bunch of three-by-five cards that say 'I have a huge zit on my forehead' and hand them out to people. You know, so they wouldn't wonder . . ."

But I finally used a small circular Band-Aid, hoping either it wouldn't show too much or people would think it was some kind of honorable wound.

I could make up a story:

An old lady was crossing the street and she fell and a bus was going to hit her but I saw what was happening and jumped to grab her, dragged her out of the way, but at the last second the rearview mirror on the bus caught me in the middle of the forehead . . .

And caused a huge zit to appear.

Yeah, that would work.

So I went to school.

Long day.

Only one person said anything about my zit. My second best friend is a guy named Nick Fleming— another name I would have liked, Nick—and he asked what happened to my forehead and I said:

"Zit."

"Oh yeah. I've got four. They're all on my butt, though."

"Cool."

"Raymond Burmeister has one on the end of his—"

The bell let loose and I didn't hear the rest because it was time to go to science.

It just got better and better.

Amber was in science and I distinctly saw her look at the middle of my forehead when I walked past her lab table to get to mine.

So she actually noticed me.

With my wound.

Oh, good. Doo-Doo the Zit Boy.

And I don't know why I cared because it's not like we had a thing going. Whatever that means.

Sure, Amber and me and my zit.

Any second now all three of us will be driving around in my Ferrari.

Day Five

Bad night.

Bad dreams.

Mostly it was my own fault. I watched one of those medical examiner shows last night where they showed people doing autopsies and finding the killer because of a grain of sand in the stomach lining. Then I went to bed.

So I had medical dreams. Bad medical dreams and then I think I wake up in the middle of the night only I just *think* I'm awake, I'm not really, and I look up and one of my posters of *Lord of the Rings* comes alive and Frodo walks into the room with a basket full of cornflakes mixed with stomach linings and a rooster standing on top crowing.

And then the rooster turns into . . .

Bad.

The bird has another feather. On the end of his left wing. So now he has one on the end of both wings, two on his head, two on his tail.

And not a single zit.

Meanwhile, he's eating like a wolf.

Plus he can hold his head up by himself now. His mom and pop brought him two grasshoppers for breakfast and he nailed them both without any help, actually held one down with his foot while he wob-bled his head around and swallowed the first one, then took the second.

Part of me envies him.

No. All of me envies him.

He just sits in the nest and they bring him bugs and he grows feathers and he doesn't have to think about Amber or zits or Frodo and a crowing rooster that isn't a rooster. . . .

My grandmother called this evening to wish me a happy birthday. A week late. But that's all right because she sent me a card with a twenty-dollar bill in it and she is very cool. The reason she couldn't call right on my birthday is that she was on a pack trip in the mountains in Colorado and couldn't get to a phone.

She's my grandmother on my mother's side and so doesn't know why they named me Duane either.

"They should have named you Carl," she said. "He

was my husband and your grandfather and a real man. He flew fighters . . ."

Whenever she talked about him she would start a story and then trail off. The memories and thinking about him made her stop talking. She never said it, but she must have loved him an awful lot.

I never met him and I wish I had. Imagine how cool it would be to have a fighter pilot for a grandfather.

So another thing that's happening is my voice.

I'm talking to my grandmother and right in the middle of the words *bird's nest* my voice cracks, drops a couple of feet and then splatters out:

". . . birrrrd neawrkst."

It sounded like somebody hit a bullfrog with a big hammer right in the middle of a croak.

The next few words went up and down and around, cracking and breaking. I shut my mouth and tried it slower.

"Grandmother?"

That came out all right.

"What?"

"I'm sorry. My voice did something weird. It's like I lost control of it."

"Sure. It's changing."

"Into what?"

"You're growing up. It's natural for your voice to change. Other things should be happening too."

Oh, Grandma, you can't even imagine. But I didn't say anything about that. I told her about the birds. We hung up and I called Willy.

"It's all supposed to happen."

"What is?"

"All of it."

"Who says?"

"My grandmother."

"*All* of it?"

"That's what she says."

"Even the ELBOW in the clouds and on the side of the bus?"

"Are you crazy? I didn't talk about that. She's my grandmother."

"But everything else?"

"Yes."

"Cool."

"Yeah. Cool."

"See you."

"Yeah."

And I went to bed but didn't sleep. I thought of my grandfather flying jet fighters and I thought of Amber and wondered how it would be if I was a jet fighter pilot and saved the country or maybe I saved just an old lady crossing the street. . . .

How would that be? I thought as I fell asleep.

You know. Without the zit.

Day Six

The birds know about me.

I've always stayed back from the window when I'm watching and I thought they would just see the reflection of the sky in the window and think it was more sky.

But this morning the mother, or the father (I can't tell which is which but I think it must be the mother because she spends more time at the nest while the other one goes hunting), looked at the glass and then through the glass right into my eyes.

She didn't look scared. Just curious. I smiled and nodded and she went about her work cleaning the nest. They're very clean. As soon as the baby could move around and balance, he would move to the side of the nest and go to the bathroom over the edge.

Which is better than a lot of humans. Billy Carson makes the gym bathroom look like . . .

Never mind. It's one thing to see it and talk about it, but it looks different when you write it down.

Anyway the birds are very clean and when I turned around and looked at my room I felt like a pig. It was a complete disaster and I thought, You know, if a little bird can clean her nest that well I can surely clean up my room.

Which made me think I was sounding like a parent. But still, I started putting things away and that brought out some sort of energy I never had before.

Pretty soon I was going crazy. Putting everything away, making my bed, tucking in the corners, fluffing the pillows—I even straightened my shoes and aligned them, left and right, left and right, and then in the bathroom I straightened and aligned all the towels and washcloths. . . .

Totally crazy.

Luckily my sister was at breakfast and that broke my mood. She's good at that. I think when she gets older and moves away and gets married—as if anybody would marry her—she'll start breaking other things. Like backs. Husbands' backs.

"You smell bad," she said as I walked into the kitchen. "Like you rolled around in a trailer trash hair salon . . ."

Yeah. Well, I thought I'd seen a hair or two on my

face and I took my father's razor and scraped a little and then used some of his aftershave cologne.

Maybe too much.

It felt like I was rubbing molten lead on my face and the fumes kept my eyes watering all the way down the stairs. I hoped nobody would notice.

You've got to love having an older sister.

Rooster, no ELBOW on the cornflakes box, quick bowl and out the door before anybody else noticed what I smelled like.

School went about like I expected.

Just wonderful.

In gym I found another zit on the side of my face, near my temple, and the gym towels are so coarse that after my shower they ripped the top off of it and it bled. All they had were these big square jock Band-Aids so I put one of those on my forehead because the shower made the small one come off. And another on my temple.

Things were going well.

I looked like Frankenstein. All I needed was a bolt through my neck and some really big shoes to make it complete. I could stagger down the halls from class to class scaring the villagers. People chasing me with torches and pitchforks. Babies screaming.

Doo-Doo the Zit Monster is coming! Run for your lives!

Just to make it perfect a new girl, who apparently

hadn't heard how terrible I was, said hi to me as I was leaving English.

Rachel.

Rachel Simpson. Dark hair. Wearing jeans and a T-shirt that said "Chocolate Forever!" across the front. Looked me right in the eyes as I came out of the room and said:

"Hi."

"I can't stop to talk right now because I don't want to be late for my next class which is down the hall and to the right so I have to hurry or I'll be late and it's not good to be late for classes and that's why I'm in a hurry and can't stop to talk because I'll be late. . . ."

My mouth opened and all that came out. My own brain did that to me. It was like a river of stupid, just rolling past my tongue and out of my mouth.

Once, Amber stopped me in the hall and asked which way it was to the new music room and I couldn't speak at all. Just stood there like I'd been shot with a tranquilizer dart. Some big, doofy rhino with a dart in his butt, head down, swinging left and right just before he drops and they take his temperature and tag his ear with a metal tag that says "Stupid."

I liked that better. Quiet. This whole motormouth thing wasn't working.

Rachel stared at me like she wondered where the volume control was located and I turned to stagger down the hall in my giant shoes, arms out in front of me, and thought: At least she won't notice the zits. But she said:

"Did something happen to your head?"

Must go, I thought, must find master, must find Puberty Master and kill him. Zit Monster must have revenge.

Arrgh!

Day Seven

You know, a week is just seven days.

Voice changing, parts of body dropping, ELBOWS everywhere, brain disengaged, motormouth in operation, leprosy in full swing—was it possible to just turn *into* a zit?—all systems in full malfunction.

Went to bed last night and lay awake for either a few minutes or ten or so years—time doesn't matter any longer. Just stages of disintegration.

Lay awake and thought—and this will show you just how stupid I was by this point—I thought, Well, this has to be the limit. There can't be anything else that can go wrong.

Right.

Woke up in the middle of the night, sat up sweating,

in horror, thinking, *Yes, but what will I do after college?*

What then?

I know, I know. Crazy. (As if everything else is going so normally.) But . . . say I somehow get through all this, you know, alive, and only slightly disfigured by zits.

And I graduate from high school.

And I graduate from college.

And I pay off my student loans.

Whatever they are. (I just heard they're awful. I'm not sure why you have to borrow money to be a student. It's not like it's fun.)

Then what?

I don't even know what I want to be when I grow up.

I mean I thought of all the stuff when I was little. Cowboy. Fireman. Somebody with a big hammer that breaks things. (When I was very little.) Heavy-equipment operator. Rock star. (I'm coming back to that one later, I think—you know, when I can sing and play an instrument. Apparently complexion doesn't matter. You can cover it with tattoos or smoke and fireworks.)

But for now . . . nothing.

So why am I worried about what happens after college?

It took me forever to get back to sleep, especially

since the bed was surrounded by snapping little terriers that looked like my sister, yapping: "You smell bad, you smell bad!"

And when I woke up this morning, guess what?

On television they said it was all a new day and everything's going to be all right.

I woke up, took two steps, fell down—apparently it's something I'm going to do for a while—went into the bathroom and looked in the mirror. (It should be obvious that this requires a lot of courage.)

Two.

New.

Zits.

One on the end of my nose. Another below my left eye.

And, oh, why not, on top, like a crown, a new cowlick in my hair. It sticks up in the exact middle of the back of my head like that bushy little tail you see on the back of a warthog in *National Geographic*.

Actually the front end is starting to look like a warthog too.

So two more Band-Aids (that makes four—and the one on the end of my nose is really attractive), and a bunch of my sister's hair spray on the cowlick while I hold it down with my finger. Then some more of my father's aftershave to cover the smell of the hair spray. Down to the kitchen. Because everything is going so well I knock the cornflakes onto the floor while my sister says I stink and I don't want to pick up the cornflakes because right then the rooster has turned into . . .

And then off to school.

Day Eight

I've got to have some kind of plan. The way it's working now, or not working, I'm just going from wreck to wreck.

Take today—and I wish somebody could.

School was like wilderness on the Discovery Channel and I was a wildebeest and every time I came down to a water hole a crocodile was waiting. . . .

Well.

First, biology. Somehow I ended up in this advanced class for science brains. Now, at the moment I *am* biology—a full-fledged experiment. Somebody should just put me in a bottle of alcohol. Please.

Add to that fact that what we're supposed to do today is dissect a cat and examine its reproductive organs.

Reproductive organs.

In my present condition, I am trying very hard not to think about those words.

And my lab partner?

Take a wild guess.

Right.

Amber.

A whole period—not a word. Everybody should try this once in their life. Stand next to somebody over a table with a dead cat on a tray. A black-and-white dead cat, soaked in preservative, a black-and-white dead cat that looks apparently a lot like a cat Amber used to have; and you stand there a whole period while the other person says things like:

"Here's the penis," or "And look, here are the testicles. See how they retract?"

I grunted and nodded but I was sure if I opened my mouth something so horrible would come out that . . .

Death. I prayed for it. At one point I had the scalpel in my hand and I actually thought of suicide but knew I would probably mess it up and wind up as a vegetable in a hospital where someday a doctor named Amber would find me and remember me as the stupid grunting kid over the dead cat and she would say, "Look, there's the . . ."

So I didn't kill myself.

And the period didn't last that long anyway. Just four or five years. And I didn't rush out when the bell rang and have Amber catch up with me to give me my books, which I'd forgotten.

Oh, no.

And things didn't get worse.

Unless you count gym.

I go to gym and find out there's going to be a mixed-team volleyball tournament.

Girls and boys mixed in two teams. And who's on my team?

Rachel.

Perhaps you have forgotten my condition, my physical appearance. Let me remind you. Four Band-Aids on the face, one on the end of my nose, hair spray holding my cowlick down.

Kind of.

As I pulled my T-shirt on over my head I felt/heard a *sproiinng* and looked in the mirror to see the cowlick standing straight up.

Like a spear as big as two fingers. When I touched it to bend it back down it didn't move. It felt like wood.

I walked out of the locker room to the gym floor to find that I was right next to Rachel.

And just so you don't think I'm negative about everything, I tried to take a positive look at my situation.

All right. The Amber business hadn't gone too well. But, I thought, if I just play volleyball and keep my mouth shut like I did with Amber maybe I can get through this day and then I will never come back to school or leave my room again as long as I live.

Could work.

Meanwhile we're just in front of the net, Rachel next to me in the corner. The opposing team serves, the ball loops over, somebody in the back row lobs it to me for an easy setup. . . .

I would like to say that I two-handed it perfectly over to Rachel and she spiked it down over the net for the point and gave me a smile like we'd been doing this for years and perhaps after the game we could get together for a Coke and maybe take in a movie and later walk through the park in the moonlight holding hands.

What really happened is that the easy lob caught me on the side of my head and, to protect myself, I hit it with my fist.

Sideways.

Into Rachel's face.

Then I tripped and went headfirst into Rachel.

"Your hair stuck me!"

And because it's Rachel and not Amber, my mouth opened.

"I'm sorry, it's because I've got a skin condition that makes my hair stand up so I had to use spray to keep it down only it didn't stay down the way the doctors said it's supposed to and that's why it stood up and stuck but the condition is only temporary and will go away . . . soon . . ."

Whereupon (I kind of like that word) I looked around and realized the volleyball game had stopped and everybody . . .

Even the coach.

. . . was listening to me.

God knows what would happen in industrial arts.

Probably something nuclear.

Man, I have *got* to get some kind of plan.

Day Nine

I picked up a three-ring binder notebook with color-coded spacers for different subjects and three clip-boards, which I'm going to hang on the wall. I have a good wristwatch with a GPS.

I'm going to log my destruction. This journal will catalog one level of it, but I think if I keep track and try to write down what I plan to do before I do it maybe it will help scientists understand how all this happens for other unfortunate souls.

Last night after my perfect day, I dreamed I was a kind of puberty werewolf.

In my dream I handcuffed myself to the bed and when the puberty full moon came up and I started to change into puberty wolf, no matter how hard I tried I couldn't make a puberty ass of myself.

Oh, I tried. In the dream I tried to talk to Rachel and not talk to Amber—both of them were standing nearby for some reason—but it didn't work. I tripped over the bed and babbled to Rachel and when my sister came into the dream with a rolled-up newspaper to housebreak me because I'd gone puberty potty on the floor . . .

Luckily I awakened before I bit somebody and spread the puberty disease.

ELBOW.

Yeah. Right there in front of me, right then. While I was writing. There's no predicting it.

I don't think the three-ring binder is going to work for one simple reason:

I don't have a clue what's coming next.

Take today. No school, Saturday, so I call Willy and he comes over and we play video games and I work on my model of an F-105, which was the jet fighter my grandfather flew. It was nicknamed the Thud and fought in Vietnam, where he was a pilot, and I was trying to figure out what his life was like.

Not one ELBOW all day. And when it came toward evening Willy called home and spent the night and it was just a normal day.

That night Willy slept on the cot that turns into a chair and after all the lights were out and we were just lying there he said:

"Doo-Doo, you awake?"

"Yeah."

"You ever think about how it was when we were kids?"

"I think we're still kids."

"No. When we were little. You remember playing with toy cars and trucks in the dirt?"

"Sure."

"Wasn't that fun?"

"Yeah. I guess so. Why?"

"Sometimes I miss it. . . ."

I had a sudden mental picture of a time when I was maybe three, no, four years old. I had a yellow metal bulldozer and was pretending that I was a heavy-equipment operator making a road in a sandbox in back of my grandmother's house.

I remembered it so clearly. I was working on a little hill and I leaned down and put my head against the ground so the hill looked bigger and the bulldozer had to push a little mountain.

The bulldozer became real to me and the sounds I was making were real engine sounds and just then my grandmother came out of the house with a half sandwich and a glass of milk.

"Working men have to eat," she said, and I was proud that she'd called me a man and I explained that I was making a road.

"What will go on it?" she asked.

"Trucks. Lots of trucks."

And for just that time, just that minute, I was a real working man and it was a real bulldozer I was running on a real road. . . .

I started to cry and was glad it was dark and Willy couldn't see me.

I knew all that was gone. I would never be able to pretend again, not in that way. The model plane I was building would always be just that, a model. I wouldn't be able to hold it up and make jet sounds and see it flying over Vietnam with my grandfather in the pilot's seat.

And while part of me seemed glad to grow, another part missed that moment so much that it almost physically hurt. I shifted in my bed.

"Doo-Doo?"

"Yeah."

"You all right?"

"Yeah."

"Cool."

"Yeah."

"We have a new girl in school."

"Oh yeah. What's her name?"

"Maggie."

"What about her?"

"I think she's really hot."

"Really."

"Yeah."

"I'm not sure exactly what that means."

"You know. She's, like, hot. Like her hair is pretty. Like a movie star."

"Oh. Well, then, I guess so." I couldn't get a picture in my mind of a hot movie star girl. Major body. A blur with blond hair cut short, maybe blue eyes. Maybe green. Somebody moving fast all the time. I was still back in my grandmother's backyard, sad because I couldn't pretend anymore. I felt like I'd lost something I would never be able to find again and that's never good.

"Yeah." Willy sighed in the dark. "She's really hot."

"If you say so."

"I do."

"Then it's cool."

"Yeah. Cool."

"I talked to Rachel yesterday." Not bad. That was the truth.

"Yeah? What did you say?"

I thought, I hit her in the face with a volleyball and spiked her with my head and told her I have a skin condition that makes my hair stand up and I had four Band-Aids covering zits that looked like open wounds and I smelled like a cheap beauty parlor or a men's barracks. "Oh. We just talked."

"Is she hot?"

"I don't know."

I really didn't.

Day Ten

It's official.

I now have more zits than the bird has feathers. He got two more on his neck, I have four new zits on my chest and I don't even want to look at my back.

The cowlick is still there but I've got all day to work on it. It's Sunday. Willy went home early this morning. I rode bikes with him halfway and then came back and went to work.

Hair spray doesn't really help. Or maybe it does. It's only temporary and when the hair springs up again it has more force. Like it's angry.

I tried combing it back and down and finally came up with a solution. Simple, really. Just cut it off. So I took a scissors, borrowed my sister's small hand mirror—first mistake—and then started to hold it over my head, looking from the bathroom mirror to the hand mirror. I didn't close the bathroom door. Second mistake.

Just as I was getting ready to snip off the few prickly hairs sticking up, my sister came by the door.

"What are you doing with my mirror?" she screamed.

It startled me so badly that I jerked, snipped and dropped the mirror at the same time. The mirror shattered and I took out a chunk of hair half as big as my fist.

Now I was a bald man with seven years of bad luck. If that was on top of the way my luck was going so far I might just as well stick my head in the toilet and pull the handle.

"You broke my mirror!"

I was on my hands and knees picking up glass and I looked up at her and said: "Believe me, that is the least of my worries. Do you realize I now have more zits than the bird has feathers?"

That confused her long enough for me to get away before she peeled the skin off her skull and became the All-Evil Death's-head that Devours the World.

It could happen any minute.

Okay, back in my room. I'd wear a baseball cap. The solution was there the whole time.

No. Wait. They had a rule because gangbangers wore baseball caps. No caps at school.

A bag over my head?

The way things were going that wasn't too bad an idea. I could cut holes to see, be the mysterious boy with the bag over his head, which everybody would of course know instantly was the kid with the skin condition that made his hair spike out who ran around slamming volleyballs into girls' faces.

I sat at the windowsill by the bird. The bird family had totally accepted me now—unlike the entire rest of the world. I could be the new bird man. Like that guy in Alcatraz who had all the pet birds. I could just live in my room for the rest of my life, a giant zit and his birds, all alone.

The baby was more sure of himself every day. He'd sit on the edge of the nest to go to the bathroom (this afternoon he caught Gorm on the head, a perfect bull's-eye) and flap his little wings like he was trying to fly.

I suppose just to build his flying muscles.

Acting as if.

Maybe that was it. I was going about this whole thing wrong—clearly. Or I wouldn't look this bad. Maybe I had to be more positive. Act as if.

But as if what?

Where was this whole puberty thing going? That was the question. So far it was just something put on Earth to destroy me. Or maybe make my sister happy. Again, all I had to do was look in a mirror.

As if I could fly?

As if I were confident and sure of myself?
As if I were Ferris Bueller?
Nah. I would never have a Ferrari.
But act as if I were something I'm not.
Act.
That was the answer. Don't be myself. Be some-
body better.
Like the bird, I had to act as if. I had to play the
role of somebody cool.
Cool.

Day Eleven

I went for it. No Band-Aids, no hair spray. I headed out to school like I was *proud* of all those zits and the bald spot. I had *earned* the right to be ugly.

And for a little while—fifteen or twenty seconds—it seemed to be working. Until I opened my locker and took out my books for first period.

Right then Amber walked by and I turned with a flourish, kind of swinging my books around while I slammed my locker door and said, "Hi, Amber."

In one fluid motion.

That was the plan.

What really happened is that my tongue wouldn't work, couldn't form the words *Hi, Amber.* Instead it seemed to stick to the roof of my mouth and make a sound like a little outboard motor:

"Nnnnnnnnggh."

While I slammed the locker door, forgetting that my thumb was on the edge. The locker door latched. With my thumb stuck in the seam.

At least it was one fluid motion.

I didn't actually scream. It was more like a bleat, kind of a cross between no sound at all and what would happen if a semi ran over a duck. A big duck.

I almost wet my pants.

Books flew—Amber had to dodge my history homework—and my tongue continued to make that squashed-duck sound and I tried to act like it was something that happened to me all the time.

Mr. Cool.

I reached around with my free hand and, with one eye closed because of the pain, I worked the combination and opened the locker door.

Gym was volleyball again and at least this time the boys and girls were separated so I couldn't cripple some poor girl.

Like Rachel.

The girls were playing at the other end of the gym. For a few minutes things almost worked out. My thumb hurt when I hit the ball but that seemed to lessen as we played.

I made a couple of good setups and then one pretty fair spike and I hoped that somebody from the other end was watching.

Like Rachel.

But when I looked all the girls were in a circle choosing teams, and missed me being cool.

The thing is I don't know why Amber and Rachel were important to me. Neither of them even really knew I existed.

Now that I had loused up in front of them I wanted to impress them when I *wasn't* such a mess.

Not that such a thing could ever happen.

We played on and I kept an eye on the other end of the gym hoping that Rachel would turn and see me at least once.

One of the boys on the other team had a smashing serve that just barely cleared the net and came in like a cannonball.

I glanced at the girls. Rachel happened to be facing the boys' end of the gym.

Just as the rifling ball caught me dead in the face, splattering my nose, driving me back and down to the floor bleeding, and worse, tripping two other players, who tripped other players, who tripped . . .

Pretty much the whole team went down and the last thing I saw was Rachel.

Pointing at me.

With a smile.

Day Twelve

Right about now I should mention that I'm a normal boy.

I mean I'm crazy, sure, and I fall over and can't talk too much to girls and I'm a walking zit and, all right, I've never been cool. Ever. Which probably means I will never *be* cool. I'm just not wired that way: to be good at sports or play in a band or say the right thing at the right time. I'm not that person.

I just looked at that last paragraph and realized it's all true. So *I* feel really good about myself. . . .

Come to the circus!

See Doo-Doo try to play volleyball!

See Doo-Doo the Zit Boy close a locker on his thumb!

But I'm normal, which means we have to mention something that normal boys do. We don't have to talk about it a lot because everybody knows pretty much what I'm talking about and how it all works. It's not rocket science.

So I have been on the Internet and seen the pictures. Sure. And the magazines. And what's happening to my body is what usually happens. Various parts function the way they're supposed to.

I'm normal.

But that's not what this journal is about. That part of it is kind of like going to the toilet: It's something lots of people do, but you don't have to talk about it.

I have an uncle who told me once that religion, sex and money all had one thing in common: People who really had them never had to talk about them.

I wouldn't know anything about that, since sex is off in the distance waiting for me. I hope it will be nice, not too scary, and won't destroy what brain I have left. I know sex is important but it's always been like a beautiful sunset somebody else sees and tries to tell you about. No matter how well they describe it you won't really know until you see it yourself. Although I'm a little concerned that it might actually *be* like rocket science: kind of hard to do well.

Religion has always been private for me.

I don't have any real money.

So.

I sat by the windowsill this evening. School had gone as usual.

I tripped in the hallway.

The school nurse saw the bald spot on the back of my head and had me come into the office to be examined and make sure I didn't have ringworm.

Which isn't a worm, by the way, but a kind of fungus. Like athlete's foot.

See Doo-Doo the Zit Boy grow fungus on his head!

The rest of the day I noticed people moving away from me in the hallways because, as it turns out, ringworm is very contagious.

You can get it from your pet. Did you know that? Or from the neighbors' pet.

I do *not* have ringworm.

So now I sat by the windowsill and watched the bird. He's growing feathers all over. Today he's covered with a kind of fuzz that's spreading into feathers.

He still looks silly. . . . I just realized that the guy who said that, me, has a thumb as big as a bratwurst, a ringworm-type bald spot on the back of his head, a nose splatted all over his face, and zits.

And I think the bird looks silly.

But . . . he does. His mom and dad bring him bugs constantly and he eats them as fast as they can shovel them in. The parents are starting to look bad. Feathers missing, scraggly looking, tired; I swear I saw the mother lean against the window to take a break.

Meanwhile Gorm tried again. What is the definition of insanity? (I'm not so sure I want to know this.)

It's if you keep doing something the same way but expect different results.

Gorm once again tiptoed out on the limb. Then, stretch, reach, miss, gravity, plummet, dent in the flower bed next to the house, stagger away. At least he did the cat thing and landed on his feet. Like somebody'd dropped a four-legged anvil. He hit so hard I heard it on the second floor, *through* the window.

Plluumppffhh!

The birds weren't excited this time. I guess they knew he wasn't a problem. They just kept cycling back and forth with bugs for Junior.

I've never seen anyone eat like this guy. Not even when Willy ate ten corn dogs at the Kiwanis Fair.

Junior did one thing that made me feel good. Or at least not as lonely. He moved to the side of his nest to go to the bathroom and when he came back to the center he tripped.

Plain as day. Tripped and fell on his head.

Puberty bird.

I called Willy.

"Hey."

"Hey."

"The cat tried for the bird again and fell."

"Cool."

"How was your day?"

"I leaned down in science lab and caught my hair on fire with the Bunsen burner. Just one side."

"Did it stink?"

"Yeah."

"How's it look?"

"Bad."

"Join the club."

"Cool."

"Yeah. See you."

"See you."

These little talks do wonders for me. Just knowing Willy is having some of the same problems . . .

Although I did make one error. For a second I felt just a little superior. A least I hadn't done anything like set my hair on fire.

Big mistake.

Day Thirteen

Let's talk about ringworm, shall we?

I thought the false ringworm scare was all over. But I hadn't figured on school administrators, parents and rumors.

I think this is what happened:

One kid went home and told his parents that Duane Homer Leech had been checked for ringworm.

And apparently that set of parents called another, who called another and yet another, who finally called the school administration and demanded to know why a child . . .

Named Duane Homer Leech.

. . . had been allowed to come to school and start a ringworm epidemic.

The nurse said I didn't have it, but the principal ignored her and brought in a team from a clinic that checked every kid in school: every boy, every girl. They used a little whirring machine and took a tiny snippet of hair from every kid, which left a little— very tiny—bald spot.

Much smaller than the bald spot on me.

Duane Homer Leech.

Who brought the epidemic to school.

Things went rapidly downhill from there. Even though there had never been ringworm in the school, not a single case, because of the rumors science teachers were instructed to devote time to studying socially transmitted diseases.

Ringworm. Measles. Chicken pox. Influenza. Bubonic plague. Leprosy. Ebola. AIDS.

We learned that a single boy could bring one of these diseases to school and start an epidemic.

Any boy.

Duane Homer Leech.

It didn't matter that they didn't find a single case of ringworm. Or that I didn't even have ringworm or any other disease.

All that mattered were those little bald spots. Less than a quarter of an inch in diameter, easily covered by hair.

The bald spots caused by Duane Homer Leech.

I'd walk down the hall and the other kids would part around me like water around a rock in a river. I was like a giant, moving booger.

At two-thirty, just before the last class, the principal came on the public-address system:

"Now that the ringworm scare is over, I want you to tell your parents that there is nothing to worry about. It was all a mistake. Even the boy who was thought to have ringworm is disease free."

He didn't say my name. But he didn't need to. Everybody in school knew Doo-Doo the Zit Boy!

The boy who brought the bald spots to school.

Now disease free.

It was nice of the principal to announce it over the intercom. It wasn't embarrassing. No more than, say, walking around school naked.

Where was Ferris Bueller's Rottweiler when you needed it?

Day Fourteen

"Look," my father said the next morning, drinking coffee over the sink while he read the paper. "There was an epidemic scare at your school yesterday. You didn't get exposed to anything, did you?"

"Are you sick?" my mother cut in. "Do we need to have you checked at the clinic?"

"Of course he's sick." My sister had three strands of hair in the wrong place and was trying to relocate them without disturbing the rest of her head. "Have you *smelled* him? How can he stink like that and *not* be sick?"

I couldn't look at the cereal box. The rooster was gone and in his place . . .

"They say," I started, "that there's a lot to be said

for homeschooling. You learn more. You can study longer and there's less hassle."

"Homeschooling? What? We don't do that. We pay taxes." My father was proud of that. He paid taxes. "They pay for the school. You go to the school. That's how it all works."

Yeah. It works really well. I go in today and they'll probably burn me at the stake.

For the first time in my life I almost skipped school. I think I would have except for Willy.

The night before I was sitting in my room and staring at the wall. Not the poster wall. The blank wall. I was ready to go backward. This whole puberty thing wasn't working out for me at all and every day just seemed to get worse.

So I called Willy.

"All right, when you burned your hair, were you embarrassed?"

Willy snorted. "No more than if I had peed my pants in church . . ."

"Well, how did you handle it?"

"You drive on. I acted like I meant it. Like I was experimenting with hair burning. Why? What happened?"

So I told him. The whole day, ringworm, disease, all of it. And when I finished there was a little pause and then:

"Cool."

"Cool?"

"Absolutely. The coolest."

"Were you listening to me?"

"You bet."

"Ringworm, disease, bald spots is cool?"

"Totally."

"Explain that to me."

"You have to think of it as an opportunity."

"Oh, sure. An opportunity for everybody in school to hate me."

"That's *it*. The magic word. Everybody. Everybody in school knows who you are, right?"

"I can't deny that. Everybody knows I'm Doo-Doo the Diseased Monster slithering up and down the halls."

"That doesn't matter."

"Speak for yourself. I'm planning to wear a bag over my head."

"Think. *Everybody* knows who you are. Every single kid in the school. It's perfect."

"Willy?" I thought he'd gone out of his mind.

"All you have to do is something good."

"I beg your pardon?"

"You do something good now, something cool, and you're in. Everybody will see it."

"You really think so?"

"I just wish it had happened to me."

"Right."

"No. Seriously. Everybody knows who you are. You do something really cool now and they'll all know it right away. It's simple."

In Willy's world, it really was simple.

But Willy's world wasn't mine.

He didn't understand what a destructive device a shoelace can be.

Day Fifteen

A word on cafeteria food:

ELBOW.

Well, not really. But many of the words the kids use to describe the cafeteria food are not printable.

The most accurate one I've heard was *sludge*.

Or Desiccated Dinosaur Droppings.

Personally, I don't really know what they have to do to actually make macaroni and cheese as bad as it is, but it's amazing. Most of the time it's inedible.

Still, at a certain time we are all herded into the cafeteria and we move down a line and this . . . this *stuff* is put on our trays.

I read in a history book that the school lunch program was started after the Second World War because so many men who were drafted to fight showed up with problems from eating bad food—poor bones, deformed bodies.

Man, if what they're feeding us now is supposed to give us healthy fighting bodies, we're in big trouble.

But here we were in line. Sort of. Where I stood with my tray there was a gap, nobody closer than four or five feet to keep from getting some dread disease.

In a way it was all right because I was in my own little zone. The puberty zone.

I'm thinking, All right, I can just go through life like this, walking along with a little gap around me, nobody talking to me, everybody looking away if I look at them. My own little world.

It wouldn't be so bad.

And then:

Remember when it was cool to have tennis shoes with that wraparound Velcro strap that held them on? I liked those.

Then there was that little period when it was very cool to wear shoes that just slipped on your feet with no fasteners at all. So easy. Up in the morning, feet on the floor, into the shoes. Gone. Even Willy, who works hard at deciding what things are or are not cool, thought the slip-ons were cool.

But the cool/fashion pendulum has swung the other way again and we are now back in the phase where we wear tennis shoes with really long laces. So long you have to double-tie them.

It is not a good time for me.

I get up in a hurry, always seem to have something to do, and with the slip-ons or Velcro shoes it was easy to just get going.

Now I have to stop and tie my shoes.

And what with puberty and all, taking the time to tie my shoes is not that high on the list.

So sue me.

Well, don't, actually.

Anyway, one of my shoelaces came untied and strung out behind me while I was in line at the cafeteria.

I looked down and saw it.

Not a problem, you say? The next thing would be simply to fix it.

And the way to do that would be to gently put my tray back on the slide rail, kneel down, retie the shoe, stand up again and move on down the line for an exciting dessert of green Jell-O filled with something that I think was supposed to be small grapes but looked suspiciously like entombed bug larvae.

But you are forgetting how my life has been going. Any little difficulty, something that would be a minor glitch in some other life, went nuclear in mine.

I mean, a cowlick that turned into an epidemic?

I looked down at that shoelace and any thought of rational action vanished.

I froze. The wildebeest at the water hole when the

lion stares him down, the impala when the cheetah locks on, the shoelace like a cobra, me the mouse.

I had to do something, but what?

I took a deep breath and started to put my tray on the slide rail just when Peter Helms, who was next in line, said:

"Come on, mud hen, get moving!"

And because he's a jock he actually broke the disease barrier and touched me, pushing me sideways.

I took a step to keep from falling, right onto the shoelace, which stopped one shoe dead.

There was a moment of scrambling, with my feet trying to stay under me, and then I surrendered to gravity, feet going up, face heading for the floor and the tray spraying macaroni and cheese, green dessert, dry lettuce and a plastic tomato slice with mayo all over the person in front of me.

Rachel.

And as I fell all I could think was *Mud hen*—what's a *mud hen*?

Day Sixteen

The baby bird is amazing. He seems to be changing hourly. Just two weeks ago he was this ugly little thing with bulging eyes and a huge mouth that seemed like it could swallow the world and now he's almost grown.

He's nearly as big as his parents and his mother is trying to teach him to eat all by himself.

Apparently puberty isn't working for him, either, because the lessons aren't going so well.

She comes back to the nest with a grasshopper and holds it out to him. When he's standing on the edge of the nest he's bigger than she is so she has to hold it up in the air.

When he starts to reach for it she drops it to

the windowsill, to teach him to pick it up and feed himself.

He just raises his head again, opens his beak and chirps.

Feed me.

So she picks up the bug, holds it up, and when he reaches for it, she drops it and the same thing happens.

You can tell she's getting sick of it because about the tenth time she just sort of throws the grasshopper down and walks away as if to say, "Let the little bugger starve."

He still doesn't get it and she finally comes back and tries again. And again. And again.

Just when I feel like screaming, "Pick it up!" through the window, he gets it. He reaches down as if discovering the grasshopper for the first time, pushes it around with his beak.

And then grabs it and eats it.

He sits on the edge of the nest and flaps his wings, almost like a rooster crowing. Very proud. And when he flaps he bounces up in the air.

Not flying. Not yet. He needs more practice. But definitely a little bounce and you can see he's surprised by it and pleased, bouncing around the edge of the nest in pretend-flight, and it suddenly brings back the dream I had the night before.

It was a flying dream. And I wasn't naked. I've had them where I was naked and that's just embarrassing; you catch yourself flying over a community and you don't know whether to fly right side up or upside down. It more or less ruins the cool part about flying. But this time I was in some kind of tights, only I didn't have a cape. But kind of like a superhero. I was soaring over the countryside, having a great time, when I went over a little canyon and saw these flashes. People were shooting surface-to-air missiles at me.

One of them burst near me and I tumbled lower before I could regain control and saw that the people manning the missile batteries were all girls. They were wearing cheerleader outfits and helmets and whenever a missile came close they would cheer:

"Die, Doo-Doo! Die, Doo-Doo! Die, die, die!"

As I started to fly out of range a close burst injured my flight mechanism and I started spiraling down out of control.

Just before I hit the ground I looked at the nearest missile battery. What do you know, my sister was handling the controls, standing on the firing platform shaking her fist at me as her head split open and turned into a fiery skull while I crashed into the ground and was covered with worms.

I woke up on the floor hugging the pillow and crying

a little, only a little, hoping that whatever career was in my distant future, being a fighter pilot was not one of the things fate had in store.

If I lived through puberty.

Which was starting to look doubtful.

Day Seventeen

This morning in the kitchen, it came to me that other people weren't living this critical-mass disaster every minute of every day of their lives.

Why?

I looked at the cereal box. Mom had replaced the one that had the rooster on it with one that had a woman tennis player slamming a serve over a net.

Not fair. It was bad enough with a rooster. How could I cope with a beautiful woman on the box?

But surprise! She just stayed a tennis player and didn't turn into something embarrassing.

This got me started thinking normal thoughts.

Again, if other people weren't having perfectly innocent images turn into soft-core porn, why was I?

As far as I could tell, nobody else had started a false

ringworm epidemic, or seemed to be covered with fresh zits every day, or was throwing trays of food around the cafeteria.

Only me.

Of course, Willy had burned his hair. That counted.

But at this level of catastrophe, it was just me.

And I got the weirdest idea that I ought to ask somebody for advice.

I ought to ask my parents.

So I looked at them: father over the sink, reading the paper, dripping; mother eating dry toast, holding a hand under her chin to catch the crumbs while she read the rest of the paper.

Sister . . . never mind. Sitting looking at her hair to see if the color went all the way through each strand, looking at each strand, studying each strand, thinking about each strand. If you opened her brain and looked at her thoughts that's what you would see: *I'm thinking of . . . hair.*

And I said:

"Mom, Dad, I have a . . ."

And I'm not sure if I was going to say the word *problem* or *question* because right then the tennis player turned into something else and I shook my head to clear the image, which for some reason made my left foot slip through the crossbars on my kitchen stool and throw me off balance.

For a second I teetered, then I went down like a

mighty oak, dragging my full cereal bowl off the counter, splattering it (*splatter* was a big word for me lately) all over the counter, my mother's dress and the back of my father's pants.

"Way to go, Grace." My sister hadn't gotten a drop on her but felt the need to comment. "Don't hurt yourself."

My mother and father said:

"Oh, Duane . . ."

Mom added, more softly, "What's the matter with you lately?"

"He's dumb," my sister said. "You haven't noticed until now?"

And you know, as I lay on the floor, I had to agree.

And then, it was off to school, "looking with bright anticipation to what joyous things the day might bring."

I read that in an old pamphlet I found at the library called:

Jimmy's First Day at School

Note that it's not *Duane's First Day* . . .

Even in pamphlets they don't name people Duane.

If only I'd been named Jimmy.

Day Eighteen

Home at four o'clock.

Nothing much to report today.

Unless you count what happened in the library: knocking over three bookcases, breaking the fish tank and scaring three gerbils and a guinea pig so badly that apparently hair loss will be an issue.

A humdrum kind of day.

The thing is, I actually had a plan this time.

I was going to go to school but limit my activity. I would walk straight to my locker, get what I needed for the next class, walk straight to class on my double-tied, carefully checked tennis shoes, sit down at the desk and stare straight ahead. Not talk to anybody. Just like a robot.

I really meant it. It was going to work this time. I was sure.

And for a while things went okay.

I got to my locker without hurting anybody. Rachel was down by her locker and she looked at me but didn't say anything. I kept my mouth shut, then turned cautiously, and carefully made my way down the hall to English class, where I sat still, listening.

I didn't take my pencil out.

Sharp object, you know.

Met Amber in the hall. Moved exactly two feet to the right, passed without a wreck.

Back to my locker.

Things going well. Opened the locker. Door stuck a little and I had to jerk it but I looked around and down at my feet—laces tied—before I tugged.

Came open without incident.

No books fell out.

I put my English books back, took out books for the next class, closed my locker carefully.

Checked my shoelaces again. Still tied.

Moved down the hallway through a sea of kids. Eyes straight ahead, step, step . . .

I was going to make it.

The next class was in the library.

Just for the record, I love the library. Some of my

best times are in that room. I wouldn't hurt a library for the world.

Through the door, past the guinea pig and gerbil cages, past the fish tanks, over to one of the study tables.

Sat down carefully.

Eyes straight ahead.

And that's where I began to deviate from my plan.

I had my back to the room, to avoid eye contact with anybody. That seemed to work.

Except that it made me face the bookcases, just five feet away.

The section in front of me was nonfiction, and right at eye level were the *P*s.

And directly in front of me was a red book with one word on the spine in large white block letters:

PUBERTY

I see the library as a place where you can go to learn things. Want to know anything, from how to track a moose to the correct spelling of Uranus or Lake Titicaca? You can find it in the library.

And here was a book on the very thing that seemed to be bothering me.

I forgot the plan.

Stood up and reached across the table, one foot on chair, fingers out, stretching my whole body out out until the mass was past the critical (and I do mean *critical*) point.

I fell forward, into the bookcase.

Which rocked away, came back, rocked away, then just gave up.

It fell into the next bookcase.

And the next.

Then the fish tank.

Which went into the gerbil cage.

Which went into the guinea pig cage.

You couldn't have done it better with a cruise missile. Books everywhere. Fish flopping, librarian grabbing them and throwing them into the other fish tank against the wall (where the golden carp woke up: feeding time!), guinea pig squeaking and running under tables, gerbil spinning in his wheel under a chair.

And me? The principal's office.

"Honestly, Duane, I don't understand this. You've always been a good student, but . . . is it drugs? I mean one day you're fine and the next you have ringworm and now vandalism."

"I didn't have ringworm. It was all a mis—"

"You wreck the cafeteria."

"That was an acci—"

"Duane, we must rule out drugs. You'd better take this container into the bathroom and give me a specimen."

Like I said, just another boring day at school. Start well, end with a urine sample.

You gotta love my life.

Day Nineteen

Stupid dream last night.

I dreamed I was at a Puberty Anonymous meeting.

I was standing up in front of a room of pimple-faced gawky boys and there were a lectern and a microphone and I was saying:

"Hi. My name is Duane Homer Leech and I am going through puberty."

Some boys said:

"Hi, Duane."

And then we talked about pimples and ELBOWS and falling down a lot, all of us with voices that sounded like broken accordions, until my sister came crashing into the back of the room throwing boxes of cereal at everybody, screaming that we were all on drugs and had to pee in little jars. . . .

I woke up lying on the floor hugging the pillow. My mother yelled from downstairs:

"Come on, Duane. You're going to be late for school!"

To the mirror. I'm not even counting zits now. They come, sometimes disappear and come back in a different place. I'm sure they are the same zits, just moving around.

I have a little fuzz growing where I cut the bald spot, growing up and out like the cowlick. Oh well.

I went to the window to check on the bird and this simple act saved me. Or I think it did. It might be too soon to tell.

I witnessed the miracle of flight.

Well, first I witnessed the miracle of Gorm trying the limb-to-the-windowsill death-defying leap again, and his plummet to the ground.

Then the miracle of the baby bird hopping on the edge of his nest while he watched Gorm go.

Then the miracle of puberty kicking in and the baby bird's stumbling over the edge of the nest and off the windowsill. Heading directly at Gorm, like a falling meat snack, wings every which way.

Gorm looked up, got set, and I'm thinking, Good-bye, bird. There was no way I could get outside and down there in time to help him.

And *then* the miracle. Above Gorm's mouth the bird got his wings out to the side and, like a plane's, like an eagle's, they caught the air and he soared up and over the cat to land in a tree across the yard.

Well, he didn't exactly soar. There was flapping and some feathers floating in all directions with both parents frantically zipping around him as he more or less staggered up to a limb of the elm tree and hung there like someone'd thrown mud against the bark.

But he flew.

First he tripped.

Then he fell.

And just before certain death:

He flew.

And saved me.

Well, not just yet. First I went down to breakfast and there was a new cereal box. This time with some kind of cartoon character on the front and I won't even *say* what that turned into except to perhaps mention I'll never watch *Who Framed Roger Rabbit* again and perhaps ELBOWS aren't so bad. . . .

Father at sink. Mother eating toast. Sister studying hair.

My father took a sip of coffee. "The principal called last night. He said there was some incident in the library but not to worry, that your urine test came back negative."

"Oh. Good."

"What," my mother asked in that occasional

mother-voice that makes you think of cobras with their hoods extended, "urine sample?"

"The one that proves he's not human." My sister held a strand of hair up to the light. "That he came from another world and was left on a rock and hatched by the heat from the sun."

"I had an accident in the library," I said, "and the principal wanted to make sure it wasn't caused by drugs. So I peed in a jar." I shrugged. "No big thing. I just fell and a couple of bookcases tipped over."

"Oh, Duane . . ."

Then, to school.

I've got to say that there was something different going on in my head. I couldn't place it at first, but there was some new feeling—not positive or negative.

Just different.

At first everything seemed pretty much the same. I tripped going through the front door of school and tore down a poster.

SPRING FLING DANCE . . .

Was all I saw as I went down in torn paper and poster paint.

Then my locker door jammed and when I jerked it the door slammed into my face and gave me a nose-bleed.

I held my head up and back and went to the bath-room, which was just tempting fate—me looking up while trying to run—and God knows how many kids I trampled or bounced off of before I got paper towels to stop the blood.

Then to class with wadded toilet tissue in each nostril.

Same old Doo-Doo.

But still, something different. Some new feeling. And I got through English all right, and the library class—although when I walked in, I saw the librarian wince and go stand in front of the fish tank (where the carp looked fatter).

But—safe through that class as well. And then gym, where the teacher excused me from volleyball and let me do exercises because of my nosebleed.

No falling. No damage.

But then—drumroll—

The cafeteria.

Day Twenty

That morning at home I had toyed with the idea of not buying lunch at all. I thought I could brown-bag it. Make a really good peanut butter and jelly sandwich . . .

But everybody was in a big rush and I forgot to do it.

I got into line all right.

Checked my shoelaces. Tied.

The cafeteria was doing sloppy joes and that made me pause. Adding the word *sloppy* to my current rhythms might be pushing the envelope.

But I *was* hungry.

I picked up my tray. The woman behind the counter plopped a pile of sloppy onto the bun. I took back the tray and then looked down.

All by itself, the shoelace on my right foot had come untied. It was lying out to the side like a snake.

Waiting.

For some reason I looked up and saw the stage at the end of the cafeteria and on the stage was a microphone.

I took a step.

I went down, and managed to get most of the sloppy joe on a boy named Carlisle standing next to me.

Sloppy Carlisle will probably be his nickname from now on, I thought on the way down.

And I thought of the bird, falling off the windowsill and then flying.

And I thought of what Willy had said about how everybody knew who I was and if I did something good . . .

The microphone!

I lay there for half a second and out of my mouth came:

"All right, that's *enough!*"

I slithered to my feet and stomped out of the line and up onto the stage and took the microphone.

I turned it on. A great hissing sound came out, then a whistle, and then I could hear my own breathing over all the loudspeakers.

Not a clue what I was going to say. Just that *I was done with it all.*

Then I remembered the dream about the Puberty Anonymous meeting.

"Hello. If there's anybody who doesn't know me yet, my name is Duane. Duane Homer Leech. Everybody calls me Doo-Doo. But I'd rather be called Duey.

"I do not have ringworm.

"I do not have any other disease.

"I do not do drugs.

"I am just having a little trouble with this whole, what, change of life thing. If you'll just bear with me I'm sure it will pass.

"Thank you."

Every kid in the cafeteria stood stock-still, staring at me, but for some reason I didn't feel the least bit embarrassed. Stupid and ugly, sure, but not embarrassed.

I turned the microphone off and put it back in the little stand, took one step onto my shoelace, went down like a gut-shot moose—or how I suspect a gut-shot moose would go down—rolled to the front of the stage and onto a table, then onto the floor.

Somebody started it in the back, a slow, even clapping, and then the whole cafeteria was doing it, laughing but not in a bad way, yelling:

"*Doo-Doo! Doo-Doo rules!*" But in there I heard a few voices shouting, "*Duey rules!*"

I was flat on my back and I blinked a couple of times before I saw Rachel standing over me.

"You all right?" she asked. "Duey?"

"I think so."

"Can I help?"

In my head: Yesssssssssss.

"Umm, sure."

"Here, take my hand." She pulled me up.

"Thanks." In my head: Don't let go! *Ever!*

"Come on and we'll find a hose to clean you off."

And she walked off while I tied my shoelace and then followed her.

The Spring Fling was a week away.

I could ask Rachel. To go to the dance. With me.

It could happen.

All I had to do was quit falling down, learn to dance, get rid of every zit and grow perfect hair to cover the cowlick.

Piece of cake.

Or, as Willy would say:

Cool.

About the Author

Gary Paulsen is the distinguished author of many critically acclaimed books for young people, including three Newbery Honor books: *The Winter Room*, *Hatchet*, and *Dogsong*. His novel *The Haymeadow* received the Western Writers of America Golden Spur Award. Among his Random House books are *The Time Hackers; Molly McGinty Has a Really Good Day; The Quilt* (a companion to *Alida's Song* and *The Cookcamp*); *The Glass Café; How Angel Peterson Got His Name; Caught by the Sea: My Life on Boats; Guts: The True Stories Behind* Hatchet *and the Brian Books; The Beet Fields; Soldier's Heart; Brian's Return, Brian's Winter,* and *Brian's Hunt* (companions to *Hatchet*); *Father Water, Mother Woods;* and five books about Francis Tucket's adventures in the Old West. Gary Paulsen has also published fiction and nonfiction for adults, as well as picture books illustrated by his wife, the painter Ruth Wright Paulsen. Their most recent book is *Canoe Days*. The Paulsens live in New Mexico, in Alaska, and on the Pacific Ocean.